INTERRUPTING COW

and the Chicken Crossing the Road

For Alison Stemple, who must have
told me the Interrupting Cow joke a thousand times.
And to Siobhan, who told me the chicken joke.
—J. Y.

To Juliane, one of the world's greatest people.
—J. D.

SIMON SPOTLIGHT
An imprint of Simon & Schuster Children's Publishing Division
1230 Avenue of the Americas, New York, New York 10020
This Simon Spotlight edition December 2020
Text copyright © 2020 by Jane Yolen
Illustrations copyright © 2020 by Joëlle Dreidemy
For information about special discounts for bulk purchases, please contact Simon & Schuster
Special Sales at 1-866-506-1949 or business@simonandschuster.com.
Manufactured in the United States of America 1220 LAK
10 9 8 7 6 5 4 3 2
Library of Congress Cataloging-in-Publication Data
Names: Yolen, Jane, author. | Dreidemy, Joëlle, illustrator.
Title: Interrupting Cow and the chicken crossing the road / by Jane Yolen ;
illustrated by Joëlle Dreidemy.
Description: Simon Spotlight edition. | New York, New York : Simon
Spotlight, 2020. | Series: Interrupting Cow | Audience: Ages 4–6. |
Audience: Grades K–1. | Summary: Interrupting Cow feels lonely because
her barnyard friends are tired of her jokes, but when she meets an old
rooster across the long, gray road, things change.
Identifiers: LCCN 2020021390 | ISBN 9781534481596 (paperback) |
ISBN 9781534481602 (hardcover) | ISBN 9781534481619 (ebook)
Subjects: CYAC: Jokes—Fiction. | Cows—Fiction. | Chickens—Fiction. |
Domestic animals—Fiction. | Humorous stories.
Classification: LCC PZ7.Y78 Ij 2020 | DDC [E]—dc23
LC record available at https://lccn.loc.gov/2020021390

InterRupting COW

and the
Chicken
Crossing
the Road

by Jane Yolen
illustrated by Joëlle Dreidemy

Ready-to-Read

Simon Spotlight
New York   London   Toronto   Sydney   New Delhi

It was another bright morning
in the cow barn.
The herd was enjoying some hay
and some cow chat.
Interrupting (in-ter-RUP-ting) Cow
turned to her barn mates.

"Knock, knock," she said.
"Who's there?" they asked
in their slow way.
They never learned.

"Interrupting Cow," she said.
"Interrupting Cow w—" they began.
"MOO!" shouted Interrupting Cow.
She fell onto the barn floor
in helpless giggles.
No one else laughed.

Instead, they all backed
away from the table
and raced out of the barn,
kicking up dirt and irritation,
and leaving their cow food behind.

Seeing the cows
streaking out of the barn,
the horses figured out
what had happened.
"Interrupting Cow!" they neighed.
And out the horses went too.
Sheep, pigs, and goats quickly
followed.

Interrupting Cow
walked slowly away from the barn.
Even the ducks had slipped away,
swimming off so quickly.
They left only a wiggle of foam
and bad feelings in their wake.

Overhead, a dark shadow
flew past, whispering, "Whooo?"
Interrupting Cow hardly noticed.
And the owl was in a hurry
to get back to her nest
with food for her babies.

Interrupting Cow
saw a single goat
sitting by the clothesline,
chewing on the farmer's long underwear
that had been hung out to dry.

When he saw Interrupting Cow coming,
he galloped away.

She walked for a long, long time.
Ahead, Interrupting Cow saw
an endless gray road,
which she had never crossed.

She'd always been content
to stay at home. Until now.
Now she was just a bit . . .
well . . . lonely.
And possibly a little sad.
That often leads to adventure.

There on the side of the gray road
stood an old rooster.
Each time he put one toe
on the pavement,
a fast truck came by.
Or a huge bus.
Or a loud tractor.

Each time one passed by,
the wind made his feathers
fly about, as if he were standing
in the middle of a big storm.
So he stepped back, and then forward,
and then back again. And again.

"Knock, knock," Interrupting Cow called
as she walked over to him.
The rooster looked her way.
"Too late for bad jokes," he said,
"in case that's what you were planning."

"My joke is not bad," she said.
"It always makes *me* smile."

The rooster thought about this
for a while.
"Maybe you have had
the wrong audience.
Or the wrong timing. Or—"
"Moo!" interrupted Interrupting Cow,
her mind spinning.

"Moo to you!" said Rooster.
"Might as well ask why this old chicken
is standing by the side of the road.
Go ahead. Ask me!"
Interrupting Cow suspected it might be
a joke, but still she asked.
"Why are you standing by the side
of the road? Are you chicken?"

Rooster turned his head and looked
at her, then laughed loudly.
"Of *course* I am chicken.
In fact, a Rhode Island Red.
But thanks for worrying about me.
I have found that
cows don't often help out chickens.

And the reason I am standing here
is that I very much want to get
to the other side.
But it's dangerous on the road."
Interrupting Cow took a deep breath
and shook her head.
"I did not mean to butt in," she said.

Rooster cocked his head.
"You've got big enough horns
to do the job," he said.
"Oh no," Interrupting Cow added
quickly, "I just meant to interrupt
a bit. Like MOO."
Rooster thought a bit.
"Any joke can get tired," he said.
"Like Cock-a-Doodle-Doo?" she asked.
Rooster laughed. "See—you just
needed new material!"

It was the first time Interrupting Cow
could remember in days, even weeks,
that someone other than Owl
had been nice to her,
or laughed at a joke of hers.
Even Owl had flown overhead
today without a word of hello.
"Come with me," Interrupting Cow said.

Rooster fluttered up to
Interrupting Cow's horn.
His flutter was slow.
It seemed hard for him to fly.
She walked over
to where a red light glowed
and pushed a button
with her horn.

The light turned green,
and together they crossed the road,
all the way to the other side.

Just before dark, they crossed
back over, two new friends
with the same sense of humor.
Each helping the other find
new material and new ways
to get across barriers.

MOO!

COCK-
A-
DOODLE
DOO!

"Cock-a-doodle-doo!"
said Interrupting Cow.
"Tomorrow I will work on finding
the right audience.
Or better timing. Or . . ."
"Moo!" said Rooster.

And they fell down in the grass
on the other side of the road
in helpless giggles,
till the moon rose
and it was time to go
back to the barn.